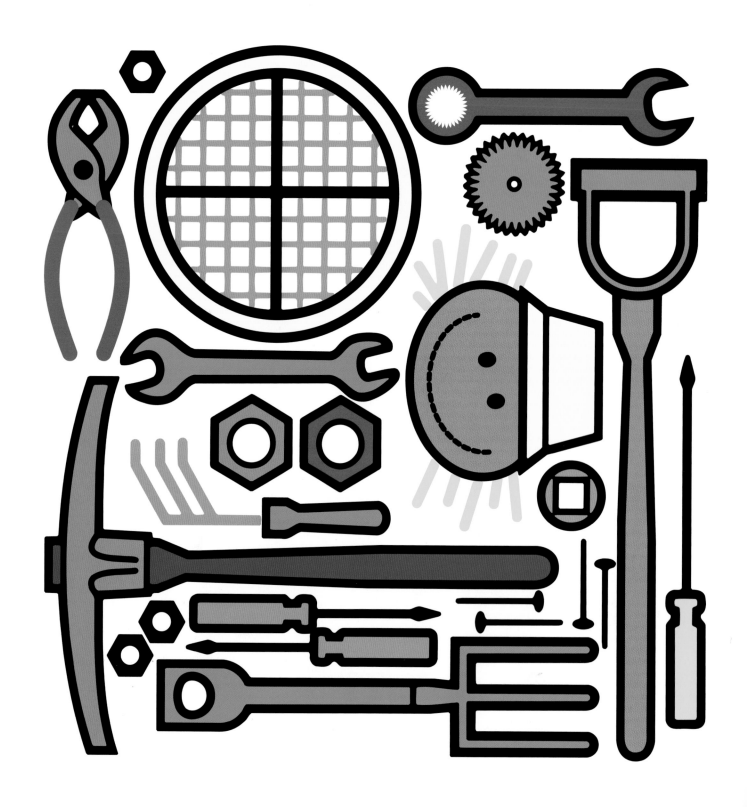

STANLEY THE FARMER
A JONATHAN CAPE BOOK 978 1 780 08129 8
Published in Great Britain by Jonathan Cape,
an imprint of Random House Children's Publishers UK
A Penguin Random House Company

First published in hardback by Jonathan Cape in 2014
This edition published 2015

001

Copyright © William Bee, 2014
The right of William Bee to be identified as the author of this work has been
asserted in accordance with the Copyright, Designs and Patents Act 1988.

RANDOM HOUSE CHILDREN'S PUBLISHERS UK
61–63 Uxbridge Road, London W5 5SA
www.**randomhousechildrens**.co.uk
www.**randomhouse**.co.uk

Addresses for companies within The Random House Group Limited can be found at: www.randomhouse.co.uk/offices.htm
THE RANDOM HOUSE GROUP Limited Reg. No. 954009
A CIP catalogue record for this book is available from the British Library.
Printed in China

Penguin Random House is committed to a sustainable future
for our business, our readers and our planet. This book is
made from Forest Stewardship Council® certified paper.

williambee
Stanley
the Farmer

JONATHAN CAPE • LONDON

Where is Stanley?
He is going to be very busy
today on his farm.

The first thing to do is plough the field,
so Stanley can plant some wheat.
Stanley has fixed the green plough
to his red tractor.

Shamus helps Stanley with
the muck-spreading.

It's smelly work!

Stanley drives the tractor up and down the field while Shamus pours seeds into the hopper.

Now Little Woo is helping too!
They water the seeds twice a day.

The wheat is growing quickly, but Stanley
is worried the birds will eat it.

So he puts up a scarecrow.
Hope it works, Stanley!

Now Stanley's wheat field is looking beautiful!

Stanley is very pleased.

Next Stanley will need to cut it all down.
He uses his big green combine harvester.

The grain goes into the sacks,
and the straw comes out of the back.

The blue baling machine makes the
straw into nice neat bales.
All finished!

Stanley gives Shamus and Little Woo
a lift back on his trailer.

Thank you, Shamus!
Thank you, Little Woo!

Well! What a busy day!

Stanley's
House

Time for tea!
Time for a bath!

And time for bed!
Goodnight, Stanley.

Stanley

If you liked **Stanley the Farmer** then you'll love these other books about Stanley:

Stanley the Builder
Stanley's Café
Stanley's Garage